Toy Town's Winning Team

HarperCollins *Children's Books*

It was a beautiful day in Toyland and everybody was getting ready for the annual football match.

"Isn't it a great day, Mr Wobbly Man?" said Noddy, happily. "I get to play a game of football with my friends."

"The smell of grass, the wind in your hair, the race for the ball and the pleasing thump of a good kick!" said Mr Wobbly Man, thoughtfully.

"Do you like to play, too?" Noddy asked.

Mr Wobbly Man looked very sad indeed. "Only in my dreams. Ever since I was Mr Wobbly Boy, nobody ever wanted me on their team."

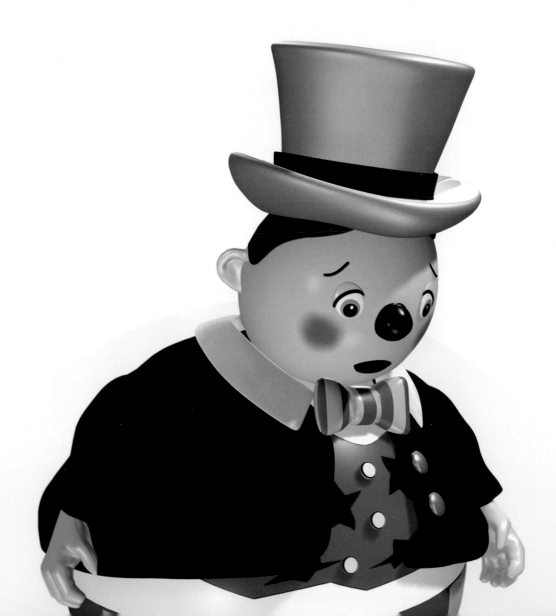

"Why don't you play on my team?" asked Noddy, kindly. "We're playing the Skittle children. We could do with some more help. The Skittles are on top form this year."

"Really?" Mr Wobbly Man replied, surprised. "I'd love to!"

Then Mr Wobbly Man looked rather concerned. "You don't think your team mates will mind, do you?"

"I'm sure everyone will be happy to have you on their team!" Noddy replied, cheerfully.

Noddy ran over to his team mates to tell them
about their new team member.

"Noddy!" shouted Martha Monkey, angrily, when
she heard the news. "What were you thinking?"

Noddy took a step back in shock. "What do
you mean, Martha?"

"How could you ask HIM to be on our team?"
Martha replied, shaking her head.

Meanwhile, Mr Sparks, Dinah Doll and Mr Wobbly Man were warming up on the pitch.

"Over to you, Mr Sparks!" shouted Dinah as she kicked the ball to Mr Sparks.

"Here it comes, Dinah!" said Mr Sparks, passing back to Dinah.

"Oh my! Warming up is so exciting!" Mr Wobbly Man laughed as he wobbled over to play with his friends.

Meanwhile, Noddy was still deep in conversation with Martha Monkey at the side of the pitch.

"Why don't you want him to play, Martha?" Noddy asked, puzzled. "Is his hat too tall? He could take it off."

"No!" Martha cried. "It's not his hat! Look at him play, Noddy."

Martha pointed to the pitch. Mr Wobbly Man was trying to kick the football to Mr Sparks but wobbled over and fell on the grass.

Tessie Bear tried to help up Mr Wobbly Man but it was no use. Each time Mr Wobbly Man went for the ball, he would roll right over it and squash it or fall over on the floor.

His friends were ready to give up on him.

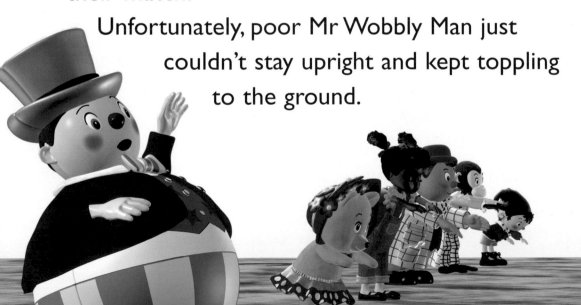

"See!" exclaimed Martha Monkey. "He can't kick! You have to have feet to kick the ball!"

"I'm sure he'll be OK. He just needs to get warmed up!" said Noddy as Mr Wobbly Man fell on the floor again.

"Huh?" asked Martha Monkey, frowning.

"Come on everybody! Time for warm-up drills!" Noddy cried, clapping his hands to gather the team.

Noddy's team mates all began warming up for their match.

Unfortunately, poor Mr Wobbly Man just couldn't stay upright and kept toppling to the ground.

"Oh dear," thought Noddy. "There must be something we can do."

Noddy gently passed the football to Mr Wobbly Man but he just rolled right over it again.

Pop! Another ball burst on the field.

"Whoops!" said Mr Wobbly Man, looking at the burst ball. "I hate it when that happens."

"Remind me to order some more footballs when I get back to the shop," Dinah Doll said to Martha Monkey as they glanced at the growing mountain of burst balls on the pitch.

"See! How can he play?" Martha Monkey shouted. "He can't even get through warm-ups!"

"Maybe Martha's right. You'd be better off without me," said Mr Wobbly Man, looking at the floor.

"No, you can't give up!" Noddy replied. "I'm sure you can help the team somehow."

As Noddy began to think, he sung a little song.

"I know a little secret, in case you haven't guessed,
You've got a special something you do better
than the rest,
Yes, you've got a special something
you do better than the rest!"

The Skittle children
suddenly came marching onto the pitch.

"They look good," whispered Tessie Bear, as
she watched them kick the ball to each other.

"They're the best. We can't afford to have
anyone on our team who can't play!" grumbled
Martha Monkey.

"Martha's right," replied Mr Wobbly Man sadly,
as he went to sit on the sidelines. "I'd just get in
the way."

The game started badly. Noddy's team couldn't even get a touch of the ball.

The Skittle children were so small and nimble, they kept running between Dinah Doll's legs and scoring goal after goal.

"I can't stop them!" shouted Dinah Doll, as another ball went into the back of the net. "They're too . . . skittley!"

"This is a VERY big problem!" cried Mr Sparks, just as a Skittle ran up and swiped the ball from underneath his feet.

No matter what Noddy's team tried to do, the Skittles just kept scoring goals.

"Do you think anyone can stop them, Noddy?"
Tessie Bear cried, running for the ball.

Noddy looked at all the Skittles running on
the football pitch.

"I'm not sure, Tessie Bear," Noddy replied.

Over on the sideline, Mr Wobbly Man had been quietly watching his friends play football when the ball suddenly came hurtling towards him.

Mr Wobbly Man quickly wobbled right out in front of the ball and stopped it from flying into the bushes.

"Mr Wobbly Man!" Noddy shouted, excitedly.
"Look at you! You'd be the perfect goalkeeper!"
   Mr Wobbly Man looked around, startled.
   "Me?" he asked.
   "You won't have to run!" Tessie Bear cried, as
she kicked the ball to Mr Wobbly Man.

"It'll be hard to kick around you!" laughed Dinah Doll.

"But. . .but. . .I'm not sure I can do it," said Mr Wobbly Man, quietly.

"Don't worry," Noddy said, smiling. "You're a natural!"

With Noddy's kind words, Mr Wobbly Man perked up and headed for the pitch.

"I'm in the game!" Mr Wobbly said, proudly. "I'm in the game!"

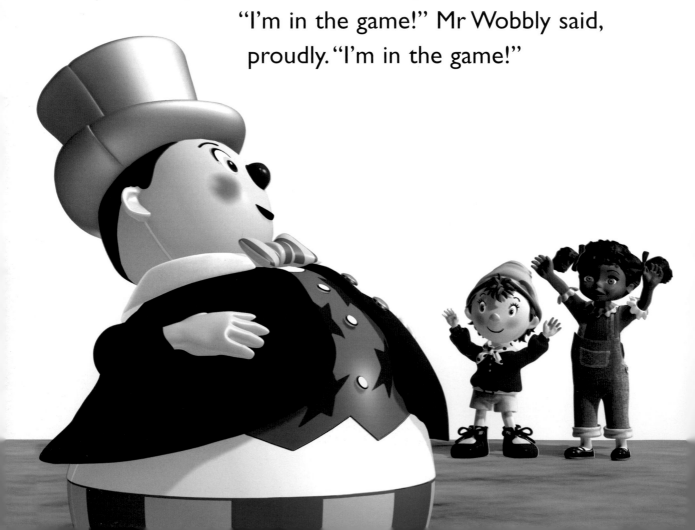

Mr Wobbly Man wobbled over to the goal, much to the amusement of the Skittle children. One Skittle ran past Noddy and confidently kicked the ball through Dinah Doll's legs, aiming right for the goal.

"To cover the goal, just wobble!" shouted Noddy.

Mr Wobbly Man did as he was told and wobbled right into the football, stopping the Skittle children from scoring a goal.

"Yeesssssss!" Mr Wobbly Man cried. "I can do it!"

For the rest of the match, Mr Wobbly Man was
the best player on the pitch and didn't let one
goal into the net. Every time a Skittle aimed for
the goal, he would bounce right onto the ball.

It was impossible to get the ball past him and
soon Noddy's team were winning by two goals.

"This is one of the best days of my life!"
Mr Wobbly Man said proudly as the final whistle
was blown.

Later that day, Noddy and his friends were all discussing the match.

"I can't believe we won!" Mr Sparks chuckled.

"It took all the help we could get," Tessie Bear said, glancing at Martha. "Didn't it, Martha?"

Martha Monkey looked to the floor.

"Alright," she said, holding up her hands. "I was wrong. I'm sorry I doubted you, Mr Wobbly Man."

"That's alright," Mr Wobbly Man replied. "I wasn't sure I could do it myself!"

"See? I told you everybody is good at something," Noddy said, smiling.

"Good?!" Dinah Doll shouted. "He's our incredible, one-of-a-kind, roly-poly goalie!"

Noddy kicked the football over to Mr Wobbly Man.

"Football!" Mr Wobbly Man cried, as he wobbled right into another football. "The smell of grass, the wind in your hair, the race for the ball and the pleasing thump of a good kick!"

"He's a brilliant goalie," Noddy began, chuckling. "But from now on, it looks like we're going to need a lot more footballs!"

First published in Great Britain by HarperCollins Children's Books in 2007
HarperCollins Children's Books is a division of HarperCollins Publishers Ltd,
77-85 Fulham Palace Road, Hammersmith, London W6 8JB

3 5 7 9 10 8 6 4 2

ISBN-10: 0-00-722356-0
ISBN-13: 978-0-00-722356-5

Printed and bound by
Printing Express Ltd, Hong Kong

NODDY™

Star in your very own PERSONALISED Noddy book!

In just **3** easy steps your child can join Noddy in a Toyland adventure!

1 Go to www.MyNoddyBook.co.uk

2 Personalise your book

3 Checkout!

3 Great Noddy adventures to choose from:

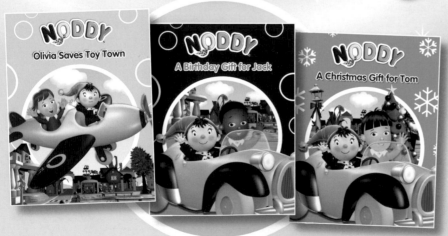

'Your child' Saves Toytown

Soar through a rainbow in Noddy's aeroplane to help him save Toytown.

A Gift for 'your child'

Noddy composes a song for your child in this story for a special occasion.

A Christmas Gift for 'your child'

Noddy composes a song for your child in a Christmas version of the above story.

Visit today to find out more and create your personalised Noddy book!

www.MyNODDYBook.co.uk